Kim Ward

Jerry's Journey

AuthorHouse™ UK
1663 Liberty Drive
Bloomington, IN 47403 USA
www.authorhouse.co.uk
Phone: 0800.197.4150

Published by AuthorHouse 10/11/2018

ISBN: 978-1-5462-9746-8 (sc)
ISBN: 978-1-5462-9745-1 (e)

authorHOUSE®

IN LOVING MEMORY OF
'GRAHAM PETER CRANE'
1959-2018

CONTENTS

Contents

CHAPTER ONE

In The Beginning

I don't remember being born. I don't think anyone does. My earliest memories are when I was about six weeks old.

Can you spot the difference?

Me and my brother Tom would roll around, play fight roughly, play hide and seek, jump out on our sisters and scare them, dash backwards and forwards across the rooms, glide across the kitchen floor and of course, annoy mum. Well, that's what kittens do, isn't it?

Tom had shiny black fur all over and most of my fur was white, with a few black patches, so we looked different. But we were all one big family.

I bet you look different from the rest of your family.

One day all our lives changed forever! A human we didn't know came to our home. He appeared very happy to see me and my brothers and sisters. Mum told us, "This human is going to choose his favourite kitten to go and live with him at his home".

"Will you come with us? We asked.

"No, I'm afraid it's time for you to leave and begin your own journeys in life!", Mum explained. I suppose it's a bit like children starting nursery or school and beginning that part of their lives away from their family.

Do you go to nursery or school? I bet you was upset when your grown-ups left you there for the first time.

Mum began licking the back of my ears and my face, "Get off mum", I told her.

"You want to look your best for the humans, so you get chosen", she replied. I scrunched my face up and pulled away from her.

"Well....I hope you do this yourself when you leave me!" said mum.

I was feeling silly now. Do your humans do that to you, get a tissue or wet wipe to clean you in front of people and make you feel silly and angry?

When the man was looking at me, Tom and my sisters we were all rushing in front of each other, "pick me."

"'No, pick me."

But the man didn't understand our meows.

CHAPTER TWO

The Chosen Ones

I was pushing in front of Tom, "Pick me." and Tom was pushing and meowing. The man bent down and stroked me. "Oh.....you are lovely," he said. When he did the same with Tom I felt something I hadn't before. I think you call it jealousy.

Have you ever felt like that?

"I can't decide!" he told the human who lived in our house. "'what are their names?" he said.

The human lady told him, "Tom and Jerry"

"That's it", he replied, "I want both of them".

Our mum said, "You must be good for the man and Jerry make sure you wash properly!" We were going to stay together. I was really happy, but we had to leave our mum. That made me very sad.

Have you ever had to leave your humans?

How did it make you feel?

The man picked us both up and put us in a basket. He took us out side; this was a place we hadn't been before. Then he put the basket with us in it into this strange house. It wasn't made of brick, didn't have any rooms, or furniture. There wasn't space to run around! It had seats at the front and back. A wheel where there was a big window.

"Where are we?" I asked Tom, he was two minutes older than me and I thought he knew everything.

Do you have older brothers and sisters, or even friends that you can ask and hope they know the answers? Tom said, "I don't know!"

Then the man got in at the front, where the round thing was. We felt a strange rumbling movement and a loud whirring sound. Then the house that we had not been in before started to move!

Do you know what it was?

I didn't like the feeling of moving, so I hid under Tom. "Get off me," he shouted pushing me out of the way.

"Do you remember mum telling us we had to start our own journey? Well maybe this is what she meant. This moving house must be what is called a journey!" explained Tom.

I believed him and thought it was just a journey in a moving house.

A little while later it stopped. The man got out. He opened the door and picked up the basket. "Ok boys we're home," he said in a very gentle voice.

'So our journey hadn't finished', I thought to myself. He carried the basket into what was definitely a house. It had doors, windows, furniture, curtains and lots more. I really didn't like the strange smell, it made me sneeze.

What was it? Do you know? (It was the smell of cigarette smoke, which is bad for children and animals!)

Do any of your humans smoke? It's really disgusting and can make you very unwell.

Chapter Three

Dinner Time

The man gently picked me up and held me against his chest. The sound of his heart beating was just like being with mum except, for that horrid smell.

Tom meowed, "What about me?" and the man picked him up. We both snuggled up with the man on his chair and fell asleep. After a nap the man put some cat biscuits in a bowl and offered them to us.

"No thanks," we both meowed. We were used to the wet food we ate at the other house. "Meow....Meow.... Meow," we shouted.

"Ok I will take the car and get some other food. You two will have to wait here," the man said to us. "Make sure you don't get into any mischief while I'm gone, Tom and Jerry."

He went out the door and we both began crying, "Meow....Meow....Meow....Meow......"

He got in the house that moved. Was he going to leave us on our own? We were cold, scared and hungry.

It felt like forever. Then I looked out of the window and the house on wheels had come back. When the man came through the front door he had bags.

What was in them? It's important when you get a new pet that you know what kind of food they eat. Your grown ups could waste a lot of money trying pets on different food, and your pet may get sick.

Tom and I were around his feet. Where's our dinner?

From then on the man always gave us food from a tin. It was wet and meaty, we always scoffed it down.

CHAPTER FOUR

The Darkness

Time soon went by and we were growing fast, no longer kittens, but full grown cats. We ran around chasing each other, up and down the stairs, clomp, clomp, and clomp. We jumped on and off the bed, bump and bang. We went whizzing across the kitchen floor. Life was great.

Then suddenly one day my whole world changed!

I was chasing after Tom and then everything went dark!! Very dark! I couldn't see anything! I was terrified and confused. What had happened?

Do you know what had happened to me?

Tom must have sensed something was wrong, because I felt him nudge me, then he meowed, "Follow my scent and the sound of my voice.....I will get you home safe".

Tom really cared about me.

He rubbed his scent glands against me and it worked.

I was able to follow his scent.

Do your humans have different smells? Sniff them and find out. Now won't that be funny?

The man did take me to a place called 'THE VETS'

Where they told him there was nothing that could be done for me. I was going to have the darkness all my life. That's alright I thought, I will always have Tom.

I never found out why everything went dark that day, but the sight in my eyes never came back.

Do you know anyone who has darkness in their eyes and can't see things properly?

It's called, being visually impaired. I know big words to remember. A lot of people call it being 'blind'. They have things they use to help them, a white stick to let people know they can't see well, dark glasses to help with pain in their eyes and most importantly a guide dog.

Guide dogs have very important jobs. They become the blind person's eyes and help them get around. Well Tom became my eyes.

We still ran around having our fun. I could smell Tom, so I ran after his smell.

Soon being blind didn't feel any different, because I had Tom, my guide friend.

The man gave me a ball with a bell in it, which helped. I could hear the bell and still play.

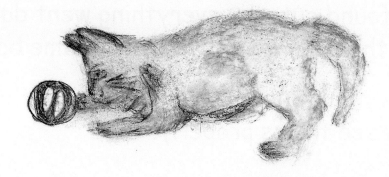

CHAPTER FIVE

Where's Tom?

One day I heard Tom being sick. He groaned "Oh.....these pains in my tummy!" but the man didn't understand him. After Tom had been feeling ill for days, the man picked him up.

"Where am I going?" Tom meowed.

"I don't know!" I meowed back.

I was so scared, what was the man doing to my best friend?

Do you know what the human was doing?

Then I heard the man go out of the door.

"Where is he taking me?........ohh......I don't feel right". Tom meowed. Then there was silence...

"Tom, Tom"

I meowed.

There was no reply.

Without Tom being my eyes I was lost. Oh, what was I going to do?

It felt like forever, when unexpectedly I heard the door. "Tom," I shouted. Nothing!

"Tom, are you there?"

Again there was no reply.

"Where are you Tom?" I cried. "Tom.... Tom..... Tom...." The tears were rolling down my face. I could feel the wetness on my fur, but I couldn't sense Tom. I screamed out to him.

From that day forward I knew Tom was not coming back, but I never knew where he had gone.

Do you know?

The man picked me up and whispered gently in my ear, "It's just you and me now Jerry!" He sounded sad. I felt the sadness too. Knowing the man was upset made me feel it was ok to feel unhappy. That's when things really changed for me!

The man was moving things around. I could hear the armchair being moved, followed by some banging. Then he moved my litter tray and food bowl. Then there was some more banging.

"Ahhh!!!!" I screamed. Not being able to see what was going on was really confusing and scary.

Finally, the man lifted me up and put me on a soft surface. It felt like a cushion.

'Oh, this is comfy,' I told myself. I smelt my food was there too, but what I really didn't like was my litter tray was next to it.

"I'm not having this," I meowed.

Cats don't like their food and toilet near each other.

How would you like to eat your dinner on the bathroom floor?

So I went to move away. Oh no! I was falling; it was like in the films where everything slows down.

I was so scared, because I couldn't see. I didn't know how far I was falling and when it would stop. Therefore my claws were out ready for the impact.

With a sudden thump, I hit the ground. I dug my claws in but that didn't stop the pain and confusion.

"That never happened when Tom was here," I meowed in anger!" The man picked me up and cuddled me.

"I want Tom," I meowed, but he never came back. This was followed by some more banging and being lifted back onto the soft pillow, where I stayed for many years.

CHAPTER SIX

Her Voice

I had stayed on the side up high for many years. It was just me and the man. Sometimes he would lift me and give me a cuddle, but the boredom was very hard for me. No-one to play with, run around or go outside with. I lead a very lonely and sad life; with no fun or laughter. The only other noise came from the square thing I remembered, it had pictures and noises. I never did know what it was called.

Do you know?

One day when I was 20 years old (that's very old in cat years) I heard lots of voices; new voices that I didn't know. There were lots of people talking to each other. I felt very confused by the voices over voices, over voices. I couldn't understand them. I really couldn't make sense of it all.

What was happening? Was my human ok?

I didn't know any of the answers.

All of a sudden the voices stopped and I was left in silence. I meowed loudly, not even the man spoke to me. There was no-one.

The silence always scared me!

From nowhere I heard a human voice that I didn't know and the silence was broken.

"Jerry, Jerry," she called out to me.

I meowed when I heard my name, "Jerry", "meow", "Jerry", "meow". I still didn't recognise her voice. I was frightened was she going to hurt me? Then I felt a very gentle hand on the back of my head. "Jerry," it was her voice.

She had a very gentle touch, and then she carefully picked me up and held me in her arms. "Oh, you were all alone, dad will be back soon!" she whispered.

"Dad...... whose dad?" I meowed.

My claws dug into her jumper and my legs and paws were all over the place. I didn't want to fall again!

I soon forgot about being scared and alone as she held me in her arms. I liked her; she was kind to me.

Do you like it when you have been scared and somebody is kind to you?

I don't know how long she held me for but it felt very warm and reassuring.

"Do you want some dinner little man?" she asked me, as she put me back on my cushion. I listened to everything she did. I could hear her cleaning my food bowl, putting more dinner in it, she gave me fresh water and she even cleaned my litter tray. As she did these things, she spoke to me softly, "Your dad will be back soon, but while he is in hospital, I will come in everyday and make sure you are ok.......... look how dirty you are," she said as she gently wiped my fur. I didn't know I was dirty because I couldn't see to wash myself properly.

For the first time in a long time, I felt loved and important. She kept her word and came in each morning, "Jerry, Jerry.....It's only me." I loved to hear her voice, have cuddles and fresh food.

I don't know how many days it had been but I remember this particular day very clearly. I heard the man's voice and lots of other voices but she wasn't there, I didn't hear her soft gentle voice.

The man got back in his chair, put the loud noise on again, then the smell that I remembered. The smell that reminded me of when, Me and Tom were kittens. It brought back so many memories. I wished I was outside running around with Tom again, just like before the darkness came. Suddenly I was shaken out of my memories by her voice. She had come back. I felt extremely happy.

"I've been looking after Jerry for you each day," she told the man, "But I have to ask, why do you keep him so high on that cushion?"

"You're the new lady next door," he commented. "Thank you for looking after him........ he stays up there, because he's blind and I don't want him to get run over by my wheelchair!"

There was a few seconds of silence............. then I heard her say, "Well, I'm visually impaired but I manage to get around! I have someone with me when I go out but when my eyes went dark, I learned to do things again!"

I knew it, she had the darkness too.

I felt there was something there, when I first heard her voice.

"Oh....I had no idea!" said the man. She told him there are some disabilities you can't see when you look at a person!

Do you think she might be right?

CHAPTER SEVEN

Freedom

Her voice must have done something to the man, because the next day he put me on his lap and we moved. We were outside.

I could smell the grass, the trees, the flowers and I could hear the birds. This was all so much to take in. 'Had she been sent by Tom to look after me? That must be it,' I thought. She was my guardian.

Every day the man took me outside on his lap. It felt great. I didn't feel like an old man cooped up in the house. I would hear her voice and then her gentle touch.  As if that wasn't enough, something amazing happened; she picked me up and gently put me on the ground.

It was cold and hard, but it felt so great, I was away from that horrible smell that filled the air indoors, which hadn't happened in a long time.

I put my nose to the cold, hard ground and took a big sniff.

It smelt like the times when I was young. I'm sure I could sense Tom in the air.

At first I moved around very slowly, although I didn't go far from the humans voices.

Do you do that in the park or in the play ground, when you are exploring? You make sure your grown-ups are nearby.

It's very important so you don't get lost.

For those last six months I was having new adventures every day; always getting into trouble. It was the best time, ever. I was walking with my nose to the ground; not being able to see made life very difficult for me, always bumping and walking into things.

One day I was outside wandering around. I could smell the fresh green leaves on the bushes, but I didn't know how close I was to them....... "Ouch" I walked straight into them and my fur got stuck on the prickles. Oh no!, I was stuck.

"Meow, meow, meow," I cried. I heard her voice, "What you done now Jerry?" she grabbed my fur and dragged me out. "Ouch!" I hissed. "That hurts!" She pulled me out and held me in her arms. I wriggled and wriggled, because I would rather be on the ground getting into mischief.

There was another funny day when I wandering around outside, with my nose to the ground, I didn't realise how far I had wandered that day. I had walked into the lady's house......... Oh!! .....I sensed there was another male cat in there, but guess what? He must have sensed my eyes didn't work and moved aside for me.

Then her voice said, "No!.....that's far enough," She gently picked me up. "Put me down!" I meowed.

The scariest day of my life was; when I was sniffing around, minding my own business and suddenly my head was stuck.

I couldn't move. What had happened to me? I meowed and a 'meow...meow...meow' came back. I meowed again and the meow came back. I was stuck and scared. Was there another cat stuck there too?

My head was stuck in a drain and the rest of me was outside on the cold pavement. Where was the meow coming from?

I tried to pull my head out but I couldn't! 'Meow'. The meow came back to me. It took me a while, but I realised the meow coming back to me sounded the same as my meow!

Do you know what I had done?

"Kim......he's got his head stuck in a drain!' my humans' voice shouted.

'Kim,' I thought, Kim was her name. She held my front legs and gently pulled me out and let me carry on. She was always there to rescue me.

My greatest adventure was my last.

I had wondered and hidden. This time I did it on purpose. I could hear everyone's voices, all the humans. "Jerry, Jerry!" They were shouting, but I was feeling a little bit naughty! So I didn't meow back, I just stayed hidden under the BBQ trolley.

They were calling my name, over and over again. Inside I was laughing.

Have you felt like that when you play hide and seek?

Eventually I came out from where I was hiding, only because I was hungry.

"There you are naughty boy!" the humans shouted, angrily. But I thought to myself, " I Kept you looking!" I smiled, I was very happy with my life.

Unfortunately, it all changed one day. I was sniffing the ground and all of a sudden I felt freezing cold water spraying over me. It really made me jump! I tried moving away, but the freezing water followed me!

"Look what you are doing to him!" my human shouted, "You are a nasty, cruel man!"

The nasty man was spraying me with the hose!

My human picked me up and wrapped me in a blanket. I was shaking with the cold! He held me and rubbed me dry, but I was still freezing and shaking. That night my human cuddled me in bed. He was trying to keep me warm, but I was shivering all night.

Then something really lovely happened. I could see, but not properly! Brightness filled my eyes.

Then I saw Tom.

"It's OK, Jerry," it's nice and warm over here'. His face was clear to me. Did I want to go towards Tom or stay with the humans that I had grown to love?

The brightness and tom's voice was stronger than the human's voices. Slowly I drifted towards the light and Tom's voice.

"He's gone!" The humans cried. "No....I haven't, I'm still here!"

I could hear them sobbing, but I wanted to be with Tom. I felt myself floating towards the light. Tom meowed at me. I could see everything. The darkness had gone from my eyes. The next minute I was play fighting with Tom.

I had gone to animal heaven. I would never be with the humans again, but I would always be with Tom.

The humans still missed and loved me, because I got sick with the cold water and leaving them had really hurt them. It's very hard for people when their animals die, but it's better than the animals being ill.

Have you ever lost someone in your family?

We all lose animals and people in our lives. At the time it really hurts and it's ok to feel sad. But you will never forget them and sometimes you may see or smell something, maybe grandma's perfume, mums cakes, grandads aftershave, a song, a television programme or a place you've visited with them. Remember these memories are precious, hold on to them.

Printed in the United States
By Bookmasters